PUFFIN BOOKS

THE KARATE PRINCESS

When Belinda, the youngest princess, grows up to be clever but not very pretty, the king worries about finding her a suitable husband. Her mother, the queen, however, has other plans for her youngest daughter, who turns out to be quite an extraordinary princess. Palace guards and cut-throat robbers should beware when Belinda sets out to bring back the Bogle from the Marsh at the End of the World.

This highly amusing fairytale turns tradition upside-down with unexpected twists and turns right up to the happy-ever-after ending!

Jeremy Strong has worked as a computer programmer, a caretaker and a wages clerk and at putting the jam in doughnuts. He is now a teacher and lives with his family in Kent.

Another book by Jeremy Strong

THE AIR–RAID SHELTER

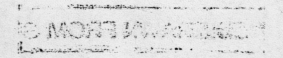

The Karate
Princess

JEREMY STRONG

Illustrated by Simone Abel

PUFFIN BOOKS

PUFFIN BOOKS

Published by the Penguin Group
27 Wrights Lane, London w8 5tz, England
Viking Penguin Inc., 40 West 23rd Street, New York, New York 10010, USA
Penguin Books Australia Ltd, Ringwood, Victoria, Australia
Penguin Books Canada Ltd, 2801 John Street, Markham, Ontario, Canada l3r 1b4
Penguin Books (NZ) Ltd, 182–190 Wairau Road, Auckland 10, New Zealand

Penguin Books Ltd, Registered Offices: Harmondsworth, Middlesex, England

First published by A. & C. Black (Publishers) Ltd 1986
Published in Puffin Books 1989
3 5 7 9 10 8 6 4 2

Text copyright © Jeremy Strong, 1986
Illustrations copyright © Simone Abel, 1986
All rights reserved

Made and printed in Great Britain by
Cox and Wyman Ltd, Reading, Berks.
Filmset in Linotron 202 Bembo by
Rowland Phototypesetting Ltd,
Bury St Edmunds, Suffolk

I

The sixteenth princess

When Belinda was born her father, King Stormbelly, took one look at her and said, 'Ugh!' Belinda's mother smiled mildly and observed that princesses never looked their best at two o'clock in the morning, especially when they were only one hour old. As for Belinda, she let out such an almighty wail that the king stuffed his fingers in his ears and fled back to bed.

As time went by Belinda lost her creased-up wrinkles and began to look altogether more attractive, though never beautiful. King Stormbelly decided that something had gone wrong with the child. He had sixteen children. They were all girls, they were all princesses and they were all astonishingly beautiful and talented . . . all except for Belinda, who was quite ordinary. But she did have eyes of a most serene blue. The king never seemed to notice Belinda's eyes.

'I don't know what we're going to do about her,' grumbled King Stormbelly, as

Belinda grew up and showed no signs of becoming a ravishing beauty. 'All the other princesses will find husbands easily, but nobody will be foolish enough to marry her. She's not even particularly clever.'

The queen didn't say anything because she knew that if she started to argue, Stormbelly would just fly into one of his silly tempers, start kicking the guards and hurt his feet on their heavy armour. Then he'd take to his bed and stay there for a week pretending all his toes were broken and it was all the queen's fault.

So the queen didn't say anything, but she thought a great deal. She was very fond of *all* her daughters and especially pleased that fifteen of them were astonishingly beautiful. But she was even more pleased that Belinda was different. What's more, she knew that Belinda was a lot cleverer than her father and it was only because Belinda always beat her father playing 'Snap!' that the king was so grumpy about her.

All the same, the king was quite right when he said that the fifteen beautiful princesses would easily find husbands, whereas Belinda would have to do a bit of work if she ever wanted to marry. The queen thought about all these things and then decided what ought to be done.

First of all she went to Belinda very quietly and whispered in her ear, 'Belinda dear, the next time you play "Snap!" with your father please make sure that you lose.'

'Oh, Mum!' Belinda didn't like losing at anything. 'Do I have to?'

The queen nodded and Belinda sighed, but the next time she played a game with her father she lost.

'Snap!' cried Stormbelly triumphantly. 'Ha, ha! You've got to have sharp eyes to beat me, Belinda.'

'Yes, Dad. I can see that,' the youngest princess murmured shamefacedly.

Off went the king, singing and dancing down the palace corridors, swinging round on the arms of the astonished guards and

making them dance with him, until at last he reached the queen.

'You seem very cheerful, dear,' she mused.

'Ha, ha! Do you know I've just won a game of "Snap!" Old sharp eyes, that's me!' He held his big belly and laughed.

The queen smiled too. 'Oh, I am pleased.'

'Ah,' said the king, sitting down with a soft thud. 'She's not such a bad girl, Belinda.'

'I've been thinking that too, dear. Do you know, I thought it might be a good idea to get her a tutor.' The queen folded her neat little hands in her lap and smiled at the king.

'A tutor?' queried the king. 'Do you mean a teacher?'

'Yes, if you like. A teacher.'

'Whatever for?' demanded Stormbelly gruffly.

'Well, to teach her, of course.'

'Yes, yes. I know that. But what's the point?'

'I know that you have been very worried about Belinda and what will happen to her when she's older. I thought that if she was taught, then she would stand a better chance later on of finding a husband.'

King Stormbelly frowned and twisted his whiskers and scratched his head and snorted a bit. They were all signs that he hadn't got the foggiest idea what he was supposed to be thinking about.

'I don't see how having a teacher will help,' he ventured.

'All the other princesses are beautiful and accomplished and will easily find husbands,' explained the queen. 'But Belinda will have to find hers with her brain, if she wants one.'

'Of course she wants one! Whoever heard of a princess who didn't want a husband?' snapped Stormbelly.

'Anyway,' continued the queen, choosing to ignore the king's last remark, 'we ought to do something about Belinda's brain to help her. Don't you think?'

Stormbelly didn't think very much but it seemed to make sense. And he didn't want Belinda to find things difficult later on. She was a good girl – he'd just beaten her at 'Snap!' and that proved it. He gave a small grunt.

'All right. Good idea. Make the arrangements and get her a teacher.'

So it was that Hiro Ono came to the palace. Hundreds of people from everywhere applied for the post of teacher to the Princess Belinda (it was highly paid), and the queen had private conversations with them all. For days there was a queue over a mile long, stretching out of the palace gates and right

down into the town. The interviews lasted for over a week and at the end of it the queen announced that Hiro Ono, master tutor from Japan, would be Belinda's new teacher.

Belinda wasn't very happy about it. She didn't like the look of Hiro Ono, with his strange silk robe that had red and green dragons swirling around on it, and his thin eyes and bent back. He had a wispy beard too, like an old spider's web caught on his chin. But Hiro Ono smiled at her, and bowed, and they went away together to begin their classes.

The years passed and Stormbelly hardly saw Belinda. In fact, he almost forgot about

her altogether. The queen didn't. She visited
Belinda and Hiro Ono every day to see how
they were getting on, and day by day Belinda
became more and more fond of Hiro Ono
because he taught her such fascinating things.

The other fifteen daughters got married,
one by one, each to a rich and handsome
prince, and went off to start new lives in their
husbands' castles. Stormbelly's castle began
to seem quite empty and all at once he realized that somewhere in the vast palace he had
a sixteenth daughter who wasn't at all beautiful but it was time she got married. He sent
for Belinda.

She and her mother arrived with Hiro Ono

trailing softly behind them, a little more bent with age and his beard a little longer. Belinda had changed too. She was slim and much taller, and her blue eyes were as clear as the blue of a winter sky. Her black hair was cut short, and she regarded her father with a little smile.

'Well,' declared the king. 'How you've grown!' Belinda nodded. 'I hear you've been taught a great deal over the last seven years.'

'Yes, Father,' said Belinda gently.

'Hmmm. Very useful thing, knowledge. So – you've learnt lots and lots. Well now, tell me, um, what are three sixes?'

Belinda shrugged. 'I don't know.'

'You don't know!' King Stormbelly was cross. He had hoped she would be able to tell him because he didn't know the answer himself. Belinda turned to Hiro Ono.

'Do you know what three sixes are?' she asked.

'I know what they aren't,' he said slowly. 'They aren't a husband. They are not a palace. Nor are they happiness. They are not the clouds enclosing the mighty head of a mountain . . .'

'What is he going on about?' burst out the king. 'Is he mad?'

The queen gently touched her husband on the arm. 'I think it is Hiro Ono's way of telling you that it doesn't matter what three sixes are. They are not important.'

'Not important! But I've always wanted to know what three sixes are! All right, then, let's see how much this nitwit has taught Belinda. Daughter, tell me, what's the capital city of Rome?'

The queen nudged him. 'Rome *is* a capital city,' she whispered.

'Oh, all right. What's the capital city of Spain?'

Belinda couldn't answer that either and Stormbelly began to hop from one foot to the other. The queen could see that he was getting ready to kick a few guards and probably Hiro Ono himself.

'Why don't you ask Belinda to show you what she *can* do?' she suggested sweetly.

'Fine, fine. Go ahead. Show us what you can do, though I shall be very surprised if it's anything at all,' cried the king, giving Hiro Ono a very dark look.

Belinda looked slowly about the palace hall. Standing at the foot of the stairs was a large stone statue of a previous king. Belinda walked silently up to it, gazed at it for a few moments then suddenly,

'Aaaaa-HA!' She gave a great yell, spun round on one foot and launched her other foot at the centre of the statue. There was a splinter of breaking stone and the statue cracked into two separate halves. Even as the top section toppled to the floor, Belinda raised her right arm and sliced the head off with a single blow of her bare hand.

Stormbelly screamed. 'Stop! That's your great-grandfather!' Belinda grinned back and began to walk up the stairway, chopping the thick wooden banisters into little pieces as she did so. Bits of wood cascaded down at the king's feet and came tumbling down the steps.

'Guards!' yelled the king. 'Stop her before she destroys the whole palace!' Up went the guards in hot pursuit, but no sooner did they reach Belinda than she sent them flying with a few well-aimed kicks and blows from her hands. Then she came down to the bottom of the stairs, bowed to her father, bowed to Hiro Ono and her mother and sat down, brushing the dust from her clothes.

Stormbelly sat down too. He collapsed in an armchair. 'Just what have you been teaching my daughter?' he managed to whisper at length.

'The ancient Japanese art of karate,' said Hiro Ono with a little bow.

Stormbelly shook his head. 'I can't believe it. Did she really do that with her bare hands and feet?'

'Of course,' said Hiro Ono. 'But karate is about strength of mind, not of hands and feet. Your wife, who is very wise, explained your daughter's problem to me. Belinda is a very good pupil. She has a very quick brain. Now she can go into the world and you needn't worry.'

'Needn't worry!' cried the king. 'I shall be terrified with her on the loose, smashing up statues and demolishing staircases all over the place.'

Hiro Ono began to explain that it wouldn't be like that at all, but the queen signalled that the king didn't understand and it wasn't worth explaining. She persuaded the king to have an afternoon sleep while they cleared up the hall.

'Well, you've certainly impressed your father, Belinda,' laughed the queen when everything was sorted out. 'Let's hope you can impress a prince!'

2

Belinda's eventful journey

The Princess Belinda was not at all sure that she wanted to impress anybody, least of all a prince. She was quite happy learning karate from Hiro Ono. On the other hand, she was sensible enough to see that she couldn't stay in her father's palace for ever and would have to go out into the wide world sooner or later.

Her chance to find a princely husband came sooner than she expected. King Stormbelly received a letter from a far cousin, King Krust. It was a long letter which made Stormbelly grunt and whistle and humph a lot. That meant it was a thoughtful kind of letter and that Stormbelly had to do some thinking.

What the letter had to say was this. King Krust had heard that Stormbelly had sixteen daughters. He knew that fifteen of them had already married and that their beauty was famed throughout whatever lands they lived in. It so happened that his son, Prince Bruno de Bruno Bunkum Krust, ought to get married and King Krust thought it might be a good idea if Stormbelly's last daughter married him. No doubt she was as beautiful as all the others, and King Krust was prepared to give his son half a kingdom on his marriage.

No wonder Stormbelly humphed a lot. It was an offer he couldn't refuse. The trouble was that Belinda wasn't at all beautiful, even when she wasn't chopping her great-grandfather into little pieces. King Stormbelly thought and thought. He had lots of ideas. Perhaps he could disguise Belinda, dress her up in a lovely dress and put a beautiful blonde wig over her short black hair? Perhaps she could wear a mask, saying that her beauty was so dazzling that she could only remove it at night?

He suggested all this to the queen and she burst out laughing. So did Belinda. That made Stormbelly lose his temper. He kicked two guards, hurt his toes and went to bed for a week. When at last he recovered he took Belinda to one side.

'Belinda, you must at least go and see this prince. He's very handsome and can do sixteen press-ups without stopping. Besides, his father is very rich and half a kingdom is not to be sneezed at.'

Belinda sighed. 'But suppose I don't like him, Father,' she pointed out.

'Goodness me, child! You don't have to *like* him. You only have to marry him.'

Belinda was so surprised she couldn't think of an answer. She went to see Hiro Ono and asked his advice.

'You must go,' he declared. 'You may not find this prince to your liking, but that won't matter. You will find that everything will work out as you wish, Belinda, for if you do not wish it, it will not be so.'

It took Belinda a few minutes to work out what the old Japanese master was saying, but she agreed to go. A few days later she set off, riding in a carriage drawn by four white horses. Hiro Ono and the queen were both sorry to see her go. Belinda promised she would return, and the king said that would be jolly nice, so long as she brought her

husband with her. The carriage set off in a cloud of dust and left the king coughing and spluttering on the doorstep.

The journey was long and tiring. Each night they stopped at a different inn and put up for the night, while the horses rested. Then it was back into the carriage straight after breakfast and jolt, jolt, jolt, all day long.

On the fifth day they ran into trouble. A band of cut-throat robbers came pouring out of the forest, waving their swords and yelling. The horses took fright and bolted. The carriage swayed alarmingly from one side of the track to the other, and poor Belinda was thrown higgledy-piggledy all about inside. First she was on one side, then she was upside-down, then she was under the seat.

Then at last a wheel broke off the rear axle and the horses slipped the traces and took to the hills. The carriage slewed across the path, crashed into a ditch, turned over twice and smashed against a great oak tree. Belinda lay unconscious beneath a pile of carriage cushions and one split suitcase.

With whoops of delight the robbers descended and stripped the broken carriage of everything worth taking. They took the royal jewellery and the royal suitcases. They took the frightened driver's velvet breeches and satin waistcoat. They took all the presents from the Krust royal family. They even took Belinda's beautiful dress and expensive shoes. They rounded up the horses and had quite vanished from sight with them long before Belinda woke up with an aching head.

She crawled out of the broken carriage and stood in her petticoat by the side of it. She looked at the driver and at the mess scattered far and wide by the searching robbers.

'Oh, dear,' she murmured. She helped the poor driver to his feet.

'They were robbers, Your Royalty,' explained the driver, quite unnecessarily. 'I tried to fight them off. I went *biff!* and *baff!* but there were more than I could manage and they took my breeches and my second best waistcoat what your mum gave me last Christmas.'

Belinda soothed his feelings. 'I'm sure you did your best. Now you'd better go back to the palace and tell them what happened. Tell them not to worry. I'm going on to see King Krust. It can't be very far now.' Her keen eyes caught sight of a dusty glitter on the road. She bent down and picked up a gold coin.

'There! Look what those robbers left behind.' Belinda pressed it into the driver's hand. 'You take that. It will get you home safely.'

'Thank you, thank you, Your Royalty. I'll set off right away, I will.' And the driver did just that. Belinda watched his departure and then began walking herself, hoping that she would reach King Krust's palace before she got too hungry.

It was further than she thought. She did not arrive until two days later, by which time she was tired and very hungry. Her petticoat was covered in dust and her skin was smudged with dirt. She did not look at all like a princess.

Certainly the palace guards did not think she was a princess, and they laughed in her face when she told them. It was at this point that Belinda discovered something. Her father was not the only king that King Krust had written to. It seemed he had written hundreds of letters, for the whole town was seething with princesses of every nationality, and all of them had come to win the hand of the fabled Prince Bruno de Bruno Bunkum Krust, for not only was he most wonderfully handsome, but he could do thirty-nine press-ups without stopping. Either he had been practising or somebody was exaggerating.

Now, the Princess Belinda was just a little bit like her father because she had a stubborn streak in her and a hasty temper. When she realized that there were at least three hundred princesses in competition with her, and when the guards just laughed at her, she decided there and then to show them not only that was she a princess but that she'd marry Bruno no matter what.

She looked calmly into the guard's piggy little eyes and said slowly, 'If you do not take me to the king at once, I shall bang your helmet.'

Foolishly the guard just laughed again, so Belinda banged his helmet. Half an hour later when he woke up he discovered that: he had a splitting headache; he couldn't get his helmet off because Belinda had put a very large dent in it; and Belinda had taken herself off to see the king.

It took Belinda a long time to find the king because guards kept trying to stop her. They all refused to believe she was a princess. By the time she reached the king there were forty-six guards with dented helmets lying unconscious all over the palace.

King Krust did not believe her either. He was a very short man, almost as wide as he was tall. He had to stand on a small stool to look at Belinda. He examined her through his monocle.

'You don't look at all like a princess,' he declared. 'You're not even beautiful.'

Belinda thought the king was not exactly

pretty either, but she didn't say so because Hiro Ono had taught her there was little point in making people angry.

Queen Krust was a little kinder than her husband and said that they might at least hear what Belinda had to say. Belinda explained carefully all that had happened to her and why she had turned up in her petticoat looking so filthy. The queen was sympathetic.

'You must have a nice hot bath, my dear, and we'll find you some clean clothes.'

'Just a minute,' butted in the king. 'Suppose she's an impostor?'

'We will give her a little test, to make sure she's a princess,' suggested the queen.

'What sort of test?'

'The usual one. We'll put lots and lots of mattresses on top of each other and put a pea under the bottom one and then see if she can feel it.' The queen turned to Belinda. 'Will that test suit you?'

'I don't mind,' said Belinda.

And so it was arranged.

Belinda felt much better after a hot bath and in clean clothes. When she went to bed she had to climb up a long ladder to reach the top mattress. The king came along to supervise the test and he stood at the bottom of the ladder and stared up at Belinda through a big telescope that his Chief Minister held for him, propped up on his back.

Belinda settled down. The bed was beautifully soft and warm but she squirmed about a bit and wriggled and after five minutes she called down to the king.

'I can't sleep.'

'Why not?' he demanded.

'The mattress is too lumpy.'

King Krust snapped his telescope shut and shrugged. 'Oh well,' he sighed. 'She must be a princess. Never mind.' He strutted out of the room and Belinda turned over, closed her eyes and instantly fell fast asleep, pea or no pea.

3

The royal quest

Belinda nearly had a terrible accident first thing next morning. She woke up feeling wonderful. She felt fresh and lively and cheerful and jumped straight out of bed, quite forgetting that she was perched on top of twenty-seven mattresses and therefore some distance above ground level.

In the nick of time she grabbed at the ladder that had been left at the bedside overnight. The ladder swayed dangerously for a moment as the princess clung to the top rung, with her legs waving wildly beneath her like storm-tossed banners. Then the ladder settled against the mattresses and Belinda clambered down safely.

After breakfast, which she ate with the queen, Belinda set about finding the fabled Prince Bruno de Bruno Bunkum Krust. She was interested to see just what he looked like.

The palace was crawling with princesses, all calling out to their servants in loud, demanding voices. They were all trying terribly hard to impress each other with their beauty and their dresses and their riches.

'Oh, I say,' cried one, 'my daddy owns a whole diamond mine.'

'Really?' screeched another. 'My daddy has two.'

'Never mind, dears,' said a third. 'My daddy has three diamond mines and a golden throne as large as a settee.'

At this point Belinda quietly walked past and said with a lovely smile and bright eyes, 'My daddy has four hundred and thirty-one diamond mines and a golden throne that is so heavy that one side of the palace is quite lop-sided. When we sit down to dinner all the plates and knives and forks all slide to one end of the table and fall off.'

The three princesses were quite flabbergasted, and one of them could not resist asking, 'But, my dear, how do you manage to eat?'

Princess Belinda looked a little sorrowful. 'We have to eat off the floor,' she whispered, as if it were a terrible secret, and she hurried off to look for the prince, leaving the princesses looking quite disgusted.

After Belinda thought she had searched every room in the palace without any success, she at last came to a huge room with giant double doors that had carvings of cherubs all over them. Belinda thought she heard voices on the other side, so she knocked, pushed the doors open and went in. There was the prince.

He was tall and slender and radiantly handsome. His blond hair shone in the sunlight that poured down through the high windows. His face was tanned. His eyes were hazel-brown and they rested on Belinda with a look that made her heart melt. He was sitting with his back straight as a board, shoulders back, in full military uniform – a stunningly handsome sight. Clutched in his slender hands were the reins of his mount – a dusty, stitched-up rocking horse with creaking springs and no tail.

Prince Bruno de Bruno galloped and galloped on his squeaky horse without getting anywhere at all, while just to one side stood a large easel, half covered with clean canvas. Working away with quick, deft charcoal marks was a young painter. He kept stopping and eyeing the galloping prince and then making more marks on his big canvas.

The prince cried out, 'Whoa!' and hastily stopped the rocking horse. The painter put down his charcoal and turned to see what had interrupted them.

'Hallo,' said Belinda cheerfully. Prince Bruno de Bruno tilted his nose towards the ceiling and eyed her distantly.

'Who,' he demanded, 'are you?'

'Princess Belinda.' The prince gave a short snort.

'You! A princess! Hmph, I don't believe you.'

Belinda smiled and shrugged her shoulders. 'Neither did the guards, nor your father, nor your mother for that matter.' The prince ignored all this.

'You're not beautiful enough to be a princess,' he declared.

Meanwhile the royal artist had stepped forward and was quietly watching Belinda. He turned to the prince and pointed out that although Belinda may not look beautiful at first sight, she had extraordinarily blue eyes, and if you looked at the blue eyes for long enough, then you would begin to see that she was truly beautiful.

Again the prince snorted. 'Hubert,' he said, 'you're a fool. Get on with the painting. I want it finished by lunch-time.'

'Yes, Your Highness,' said Hubert the artist, with a short bow, and he returned to his easel and canvas.

Belinda watched the prince for a little longer. She decided he was rather rude, but

no doubt that was because he was a prince. There was certainly no doubt that he was handsome, although she hadn't yet seen him do any press-ups. Besides, if he didn't think very much of her, then she would have to make sure that he changed his mind.

She left the prince, creaking away on his galloping rocking horse, and went off to find a quiet little room for herself, where she could do some thinking and planning. On the way she passed a big hall mirror, and she couldn't resist stopping quickly to take a look at her eyes. Nobody had ever said they were beautiful before. In the mirror they sparkled back at her, but Belinda could not see why they were beautiful at all. She thought they were just like . . . well, like eyes.

In the meantime, King Krust was having a bit of a problem. He was sitting up in bed, surrounded by his most important ministers. The king always held his most important meetings when he was in bed because his ministers made such long speeches he kept dropping off to sleep. If you're going to drop off to sleep, he pointed out, you may as well be in bed and do it properly.

'We've got a problem,' he announced.

'Yes, Your Majesty.'

'To put it another way, we've got four hundred and three problems, because that's how many princesses there are. They're cluttering up the palace and eating me out of house and home.'

'Yes, Your Majesty,' nodded the old and important ministers.

'Well, what are we going to do about it?' the king snapped.

A chorus of ums and ahs filled the royal bedchamber. One minister pressed his fingertips together one by one and coughed.

'I suppose we could poison them,' he said.

'That's a good idea. That would get rid of them,' said the others.

King Krust sighed. 'It is not a good idea at all. What do you think would happen when their fathers found out? They'd all be coming round here, waving their swords and things. No, no. We can't have that.'

There was a long silence, during which the king began to snore. He jerked awake. 'The whole point is,' he grunted, 'we are trying to find a wife for my son. How on earth do we choose the right wife out of all that lot?'

'Perhaps we could give them numbers and draw one out of a hat?'

'Don't be so stupid!' he snapped, seizing his crown and holding it out for all to see. 'How can you put numbers in that? They'd go straight through!'

The other important ministers glared at

the unlucky one who had made the suggestion. 'How stupid!' they grumbled. Then
another one had a good idea.

'Your Majesty, suppose we gave all the
princesses a task to complete. Then whoever
did it first could marry your son.'

At first there was no reply because King
Krust was fast asleep again. The poor minister had to repeat his suggestion all over again.

'Hmmm,' mumbled the king. 'That might
work. What sort of task?'

'Well, I need some buttons sewn on my
shirt,' one suggested.

'My lawn needs mowing,' said another.

'I say, I left my poor wife with her big toe
stuck in the bath tap. I don't know how she's
going to get it out.'

'Saw her leg off!' cried the king, standing
up in his bed and waving his little arms
about. 'This is ridiculous. They should be
fighting dragons or something, not sewing
on buttons and pulling toes out of bath taps.'

'Yes, Your Majesty, but we don't have any
dragons.'

One of the more silent ministers mumbled
something about his wife being rather fierce,
but nobody heard him.

'We must have something dangerous
somewhere in the kingdom,' said the king,
sitting down again.

'Your Majesty, I believe we do have a Bogle somewhere. Hiding in the Marsh at the End of the World, I think.'

'My goodness, that's a long way off. That's probably why I've never heard of it before. What on earth is a Bogle?' King Krust snuggled down under the bedcovers as if he expected a bedtime story.

'Bogles are a bit like men,' explained the important minister. 'But they are very hairy and have long arms, long fingers and even longer fingernails.'

'Ugh,' said the king.

'Quite so, Your Majesty. Their eyes glow in the dark, and they have hair sprouting out of their nostrils and ears. They are not very pretty,' added the minister, quite un-necessarily.

'No, well, I wasn't thinking of inviting him to my birthday party, you know. Tell me what they eat.'

'Slugs and beetles, Your Majesty, but if they could, they would eat humans. Every so often they come out of the marsh and seize a few people. They're never ever heard of again.'

King Krust clapped his hands. 'Just the job,' he said. 'He'll do nicely. Has he got a name, this Bogle?'

'I believe he's known as Knackerleevee.'

'Good, good, good,' said the king, jump-ing out of bed. 'Get the princesses together and I shall be down shortly.'

It took the king three hours to get himself dressed, partly because he couldn't be bothered to undo his cuff buttons and conse-quently his arms got stuck in his shirt sleeves. When at last he arrived in the main hall he found it jam-packed with the princesses. The noise was awful.

A big gong sounded, and King Krust raised his arms.

'Silence, silence!' he yelled. 'I have an announcement. Now, you have all come here to marry my wonderful son, Prince

Bruno de Bruno Bunkum Krust.' Here there were great cheers and a curtain was pulled back to reveal the portrait that Belinda had seen earlier that morning. The paint was still wet, but there for all to see was Bruno de Bruno, dashing across the countryside on a magnificent white horse. Belinda, who was crushed right at the back of the hall, couldn't help thinking it was a shame that nobody else had seen the stitched-up rocking horse.

Several princesses swooned at the sight of the handsome prince and had to be carried from the room, to be dumped in a passage outside. The king continued.

'Now, there are far too many princesses to marry my son – that honour can fall to only one of you. I have therefore arranged for a competition. Whoever completes this task will marry my son and receive half my kingdom . . . but not the bit with the diamond mine. I'm having that half. At the far corner of my kingdom, in the Marsh at the End of the World, there lives a Bogle. His name is Knackerleevee. He is very hairy, smells of fish and eats people. I want him brought back, dead or alive.'

At this announcement a whole lot more of the princesses swooned away at the thought of smelly fish. Another couple of hundred took to their heels and ran out of the palace,

never to be seen again. In short, only two princesses were left, standing all alone in the big hall.

The king could hardly believe his eyes. It was wonderful. All the princesses had gone at last. He stared down at the two left behind.

'I know you,' he said to Belinda, 'but who are you?'

The second princess, who was, naturally, astonishingly beautiful, stepped forward and gave the king a dazzling smile.

'Your Majesty,' she crooned. 'I am the Princess Saramanda Sneak, and I shall bring you the Bogle dead or alive, just as you wish.'

The princess bent over his hand and gave it a sloppy kiss. King Krust turned to his important ministers with a beaming face.

'There,' he said. 'I think that was an excellent idea of mine!' And he added in a loud whisper that Belinda heard quite clearly, 'I do hope Saramanda wins. Isn't she a stunner? I don't fancy that other one as a daughter-in-law at all.'

4

Princess Saramanda Sneak

Belinda was eager to start off straight away for the Marsh at the End of the World, but King Krust was in no particular hurry.

'You may as well stay for tea,' he said. 'And then it will be too late to start before nightfall, so you may as well spend the night here and set off in the morning.'

The truth of the matter was that he liked looking at Princess Saramanda. After all, she was a rather stunning creature, with sparkling gold hair that flowed right down to her waist. It glittered with tiny gems.

The queen wasn't too pleased to see her husband staring at this new princess.

'I don't think that Salamander girl is very nice,' she said, in private, to her husband.

'Not Salamander dear, Saramanda. A salamander is a kind of blotchy lizard, I think.'

'Exactly. I don't trust lizards and I don't trust her either.'

King Krust began to waddle quickly round and round the room.

'And I don't think much of that Belinda person either. She comes here in her petticoat with mud all over her face. She uses our dresses and sleeps in our beds, not to mention half killing the guards. Do you know that most of them are still in hospital? I mean to say, what kind of princess goes around clonking guards on the head?'

The queen shrugged. 'Quite honestly I have often felt like doing that myself,' and she gave her husband a withering look which he pretended he hadn't seen.

In fact, the queen was quite right to mistrust the Princess Saramanda, even if she did so for the wrong reasons. The princess was very pretty to look at, but inside her pretty head was a very mean brain. Saramanda was constantly dreaming up wicked plots. At the age of three she cheated her two older brothers out of their dinners for a whole week. By the time she was eleven she had caused a war between her father's kingdom and their neighbour's, by kidnapping the neighbour's favourite poodle and refusing to return it until a large ransom had been paid.

Saramanda wished to marry Bruno de Bruno more than anything else in the world. She realized that when King Krust died, his son would inherit the rest of the kingdom anyway, and then she would be queen and she would have the half with the diamond mine too. Saramanda was very fond of diamonds and would do anything to get her slender fingers on them. She even employed her own band of robbers who went about the countryside taking diamonds from anybody who had them. But, being robbers, they took everything else as well. They handed the diamonds over to the princess and kept the rest for themselves. These were the robbers who had stolen Belinda's things on her way to King Krust's castle.

That night Princess Saramanda slept very well, dreaming up different ways of getting rid of Belinda and winning Bruno de Bruno – such a handsome chap too. She adored tall, strong men with big shoulders and blond hair. No doubt he would shower her with diamonds.

The following morning King Krust came to the palace gateway to see the two princesses off. A grand assembly of important people had gathered around the prancing horses. Belinda and Saramanda eyed each other. Then the royal painter came along, sitting in a small cart loaded high with canvas and easels and pots and pots of paint.

'He's going too,' explained the king. 'I want a nice picture of the battle for the Great Hall. There's a horrible splodge on the wall

where the queen threw her rice pudding at me last year, and I've been wondering how to cover it up. A big picture of a Bogle Battle will do me nicely.' The king turned to the royal artist. 'Make sure there's lots of blood and everything in it, Hubert.'

'Yes, Your Majesty.'

Princess Saramanda smiled sweetly down from her horse. 'I do hope it's not our blood, Your Majesty!'

He widened his eyes. 'Oh, my goodness, no. At least, not your blood, you little fairy cloud!'

These words did not give Belinda much hope, but at that moment she caught sight of Prince Bruno de Bruno, standing alone on a high balcony and watching them. The wind fluttered through his golden locks and he stared down at them with his hazel eyes, his strong jaw jutting out as proud as a ship cleaving the waves.

She turned her lively horse, waved good-bye and cantered away towards the Marsh at the End of the World. Hubert the painter gave his old horse a prod with a paint brush, and the cart rumbled after her.

Princess Saramanda watched them both go, a smile on her lips.

'Keep going, dear Belinda!' she whispered to herself. 'I've arranged a little party for you – a party of robbers. With a bit of luck that royal painter might meet with an unfortunate accident too.' So saying, she blew a kiss at the king, who immediately turned bright red and almost fell off his royal stool. She then rode slowly after Belinda and Hubert.

It was a lovely day. The sun was splendid above, and the clear sky matched the brilliance of Belinda's eyes – not that she realized that, of course, as she trotted cheerfully through the woods and fields.

Not far behind came Hubert, humming softly to himself and trying to decide if Belinda's eyes should be cobalt blue or cyan. 'Cobalt is too blue,' he said to himself. 'And cyan is a shade too light, so I shall mix them both together and that should be about right.

I'll call it Belinda blue.' This thought seemed to make him even happier and he began to sing in a loud, strong voice. The old horse joined in too, and they made so much noise together that at first they didn't hear the shouts and bangs and yells that were coming from the wood just ahead.

Saramanda's robbers had decided it was time to swoop down on poor Belinda. Saramanda had said they could do what they liked with her. Perhaps they might like to ransom her, or if they couldn't be bothered with all that trouble, they might prefer to kill her – if they got the chance!

As soon as Belinda saw the twenty or so robbers hurtling down the hillside towards her, she realized they were the very same robbers who had robbed her once before. She pulled in her horse sharply and jumped lightly to the ground. She tied her horse safely to a tree and then stood in a large clearing where the robbers could see her quite plainly.

'I'm getting fed up with this,' she muttered. 'Wherever I go there's trouble. I wish Hiro Ono was with me. Never mind, there are only about twenty of them.'

By this time the robbers were pounding through the trees, whooping and shouting and waving great curved swords over their heads. One of them managed to chop the feather off his own hat, he was so excited. They circled round Princess Belinda, laughing away like the jolly robbers they were.

'What shall we do with her, mateys?' cried their leader, a big fat robber with a black beard like sofa-stuffing.

'Chop off her head!'

'Chop off her legs!'

And they all began to chant.

'Chip, chop, chop off her legs! Chip, chop, chop off her head!'

They got down from their horses and poked their swords at Belinda and marched round and round, still chanting away. Belinda stood quite still and calmly watched each one.

Hubert the painter had heard all the singing, and he drove his cart into the woods to see what was going on. He was horrified. There was poor little Belinda, surrounded by nasty robbers. Hubert felt helpless. 'I'm helpless Hubert,' he thought. He wanted to cover his eyes, for he hardly dared to look. But if he didn't look, he wouldn't know what was going to happen. So he covered his eyes and parted his fingers so he could see between them.

He saw the big, fat chief robber rush up to

Belinda with his flashing sword. A moment later the sword lay in two pieces and the robber chief was stuck in a tree, trying to get his breath back. Hubert rubbed his eyes in disbelief. Then two more robbers rushed furiously upon little Belinda. She spun on one heel, knocked one senseless with a flying kick to the jaw and crammed the other's helmet so far down on his head that his skull came poking out of the top. He staggered off among the trees.

The robbers realized that Belinda was no ordinary princess. They banded together in a big bunch and then charged at her, snarling and snapping like mad dogs. For several seconds Hubert could not see what was happening. Everybody was rushing hither and thither. Dust clouds burst all around the skirmishing robbers, and the yells and bangs and clangs were enough to deafen a snake. Since snakes don't have ears, you can imagine how loud it all was.

Hubert crouched behind his tree and watched. First one robber came flying out of the cloud of dust and landed in a still heap, then two more staggered out, clutching their stomachs and holding each other up. Another robber went hurtling up into a tree and landed alongside the robber chief. A fifth robber came spinning out of the fight like some gigantic flying starfish. He hit a tree trunk and sank to the ground.

Suddenly it was all over. The remaining robbers dashed to their horses and disappeared, yelping, over the horizon. As the dust settled, Hubert at last saw Princess Belinda. She was brushing a smudge of dirt off one shoulder.

'Oh, look,' she said to Hubert as he came creeping up to her in utter amazement, 'I've got some dirt on this dress and it's not even mine.'

Hubert was speechless. He pointed in silence at the groaning robbers all about them. 'How did you do it?' he croaked. Belinda laughed and took a step closer.

'I'll show you, shall I?'

Hubert almost jumped out of his skin.

'No, no. It's quite all right. It was wonderful. I've never seen anything like it.'

There was a sound of approaching hooves and the Princess Saramanda trotted into sight. Her face turned white at the spectacle of half her robbers lying bruised and broken on the ground – not to mention the two stuck up a tree.

Hubert rushed eagerly to Saramanda and told her all that he had seen. Princess Saramanda was seething with fury inside, but she smiled sweetly at Belinda and said in her oh-so-soft voice, 'My, my, you have got a temper, haven't you? Well, see you at the Marsh at the End of the World!' And she rode on. Saramanda was not furious for long. A rather nice thought came into her head. She had been wondering all along how to catch the Bogle and now she knew what to do.

'I'll let that dear little muscle-bag Belinda catch him. She can do all the hard work and I shall do the easy bit – taking the Bogle back to the castle and marrying Bruno!'

5

The Bogle

The Marsh at the End of the World was the most dismal place that Princess Belinda had ever seen. Swirling mists drifted over grey tussocks of dirty grass. Dark pools of stagnant, scummy water were pimpled with bubbles. They would slowly grow until they at last burst with a muffled *plop!* and a nauseating stink would fill the air.

Belinda stood on the edge, with the mud seeping over her shoes. She peered anxiously into the mist. Hubert left the heavy cart at a safe distance, then came sloping over.

'It's not very pretty, is it?' he said mournfully. 'I don't know what King Krust will think if I paint a picture of this. It's all dirty grey and green – and the smell is terrible.'

Belinda smiled and looked at the royal painter, who was busily smothering his sensitive nose with a large, grubby handkerchief.

'You can't paint a smell,' she said.

'I thought I'd be able to paint some nice

landscapes,' complained Hubert. 'Views of shining mountains and trees waving in the wind. I hate painting people, especially King Krust. He just gets fatter, and the queen always complains that I've made her nose too large. I'm much better at landscapes, you know. But this – it's just green: grey-green, dark green, grass-green, mid-green, green, green and more green. It's utterly, greenly boring.' The painter heaved a sigh and plodded back to the cart to unload his materials.

Belinda was glad to be left alone. She was nervous. She did not know what might be out in the marsh, lurking, ready to pounce. She knew only that she had to enter the mist and the mire and find the Bogle. Princess Saramanda might already be in there.

Belinda tried not to think of her fears as she plunged resolutely into the marsh. Soon her feet were sinking down into the oozing mud, and sometimes she sank right up to the waist. She tried to keep near the big mounds of grass and managed to pull herself out by hauling on the thick grass.

There was the stench too, as she disturbed all the old, stagnant pools. It was very unpleasant, but could not be avoided. She was covered with the foul-smelling mud and looked as if a wet and sloppy cow field had

suddenly exploded as she was walking through it.

At length she came to a halt. She climbed on to a big mound of grass and stood there, panting, shivering and lost. Around her the mist slowly ribboned out across the marsh. Not a sound was to be heard, except the slow plopping of the bubbles of gas. Nor was there anything to be seen save the grey-green wasteland stretching in every direction.

The chill of the marsh-water seeped into Belinda's bones, and a horrid fear began to creep into her heart. She cupped her hands to her mouth.

'Knackerleevee! Knackerleevee!' Her voice died away on the marsh wind. A bubble rose and burst and Belinda held her nose.

'Knackerleevee! Bogle! I am the Princess

Belinda and have come to fight you. You Bogle-buffoon!'

Again there was silence. Belinda peered through the mists. Sometimes she thought she saw a huddled shape moving, then it would vanish. The silence was sinister. She cupped her hands once more, then heard it – a faint splashing, far away at the back of the marsh. 'Knackerleevee!' she yelled. 'I'm over here, you great oaf!'

The splashes came nearer and a grumbling, raspy old voice drifted through the mist. 'Great oaf, am I? Bogle-buffoon? What kind of fool would call Knackerleevee a buffoon? It must be a king-sized, cross-eyed fool!' A grey, hunched shape began to appear through the mist, plunging carelessly through the puddles. 'And fools always make very good sandwiches,' the Bogle went on, talking mostly to himself now.

He came nearer and nearer, grunting softly as he plodded towards Belinda. Her serene sky-blue eyes grew larger and rounder as she began to make out his truly huge shape, moving through the mists like some monstrous human dinosaur. A chill fear numbed her brain and froze her muscles.

Out of the mist came Knackerleevee, his small eyes glowing a nasty pink-red colour. His wide, flared nostrils quivered with clumps of black hair. His chest was swaddled with muscle and so much wiry hair that he resembled a walking doormat. The Bogle stopped a few paces away from the princess and began to smile. It was a slow smile that ended up showing all his teeth – big, black and sharp.

'I'm Knackerleevee,' he growled. 'And I eat princesses for my tea, when I can find them.' An expression of disgust twisted his long and crooked mouth into an ugly knot. He rolled his red eyes and smashed one hairy fist into a pool. Brown water sprayed into the air. 'I don't see much point in eating you! You're too skinny, and I dare say you taste of jasmine perfume.' The Bogle spat loudly into the marsh. 'The last princess I ate tasted of jasmine perfume. She tasted foul, but at least she had a bit of meat on her!' He reached out with surprising speed and felt Belinda's left arm. 'Ugh – it's like string. Why don't they make fat princesses any more?' And Knackerleevee grunted and snorted, picked his nose and glared steadily at Belinda with his little red eyes.

Now, Belinda's heart was thumping away like one of those road–flatteners, but Hiro Ono had taught her well. 'Always stay calm,' he had told her. 'There is nothing that frightens the enemy more than calmness.

Muscles and weapons are nothing so long as you show no fear.' So although her insides were running away into every possible corner to hide, outwardly Belinda appeared calm and untroubled.

'Well,' she said, 'as a matter of fact I haven't come here so that you can eat me. I've come to defeat you in battle.'

Knackerleevee banged his fists on his knees and then on his head – which made his eyes water quite a lot – and roared with laughter. 'You couldn't fight me!' he yelled. 'You're just a skinny girl. Princesses don't fight!' He thrust his face up against hers and growled. 'They get eaten! I could break you into so many pieces it would take a year to find them all. I could throw you so far you'd probably never even land anywhere. You fight me? Ha!'

Princess Belinda began to redden. She was getting fed up with all this nonsense. She angrily dragged an old log from the marsh and stuck it upright in front of her. It was as thick as one of Knackerleevee's legs. The Bogle narrowed his eyes and rasped, 'Now what are you trying to do?'

Belinda took a deep breath and concentrated. 'Haaaaaa – akk!' Her fist sliced the air. There was a dull *crack!* and the top half of the log toppled over and fell with a splash into the marsh. Belinda straightened up, glanced quietly at the Bogle and bowed.

Knackerleevee stuck out his bottom lip and dribbled thoughtfully. Then he grunted down his nose and pulled another thick log from the marsh and set it upright. He glared nastily at Belinda and then at the log and cried out,

'Urrrr – UNK!' He smashed his fist into the log and leapt away screaming, 'Owwwwowowowooooooarhowow,' with his fist jammed under his other arm and hopping from one leg to the other.

'It took me a long time to learn how to do that,' said Belinda gravely. 'You should never try such things without proper training.'

The Bogle sank down on to a mound and nursed his fist. He was broken and dejected. His jaw drooped on to his chest, and he regarded Belinda with such pale and sorrowful eyes that if she wasn't sure he was a big, brave Bogle, she would have thought he was crying.

'It can't be,' he moaned. 'I eat princesses . . .' He glanced up at Belinda. 'I *used* to eat princesses. How did you do it? Such strength from such a little person.'

'It's called karate, and it took me seven years to learn.' Belinda paused and studied the dejected creature in front of her. 'Look, does this mean that you're not even going to fight me?'

Knackerleevee recoiled in horror. 'Fight you! No, never!' He suddenly threw himself at Belinda's feet in a muddy huddle. 'No, princess! Don't fight me, but teach me karate! Teach me how to do that thing with the log.'

Belinda's insides had stopped running away to hide and were rushing back to their proper places, giggling madly. Outwardly she remained calm – it wouldn't do for a princess to giggle in front of a Bogle.

'Teach me karate, Your High Royalship,' pleaded Knackerleevee.

'You'll have to come with me,' said Belinda sharply.

'I will, I will.'

'Wherever I go?'

'Wherever you go, Royalness. I shall follow you everywhere if only you will teach me the secret of your strength.'

Belinda reached down and touched the Bogle for the first time. His skin was hairy and caked with mud, but it was warm and soft underneath. 'I don't think you're such a bad beast after all,' she said. The Bogle gazed up at her with grateful eyes.

'Everybody's got to eat something,' he pointed out.

'Hmmm. I think eating people is a bit much, you know.'

'But they taste so nice, Princess! Especially the legs!'

'Even when they're like string?' suggested Belinda. Knackerleevee lowered his eyes, mortified.

'I'm sorry I was so rude,' he stammered.

'Oh, come on, you big lump! Stop being so gloomy. Get up and show me the way out of this horrible place.'

Knackerleevee dragged himself out of the mud. He swung Belinda up on to his shoulders to ride in triumph, and together they set off for dry land.

'We must find Hubert,' hiccuped Belinda, who was getting rather bounced about on the Bogle's massive shoulders.

'Who's Hubert, Your Royalshipness?' asked the Bogle, splashing through the marsh.

'He's an artist, and he's rather sensitive, so try not to upset him. Oh, and Knackerleevee?'

'Yes, O Royalshipnesty?'

'My name is Belinda, and if you call me a royal whatsit once more, I shall give you a demonstration of karate on your head. Do you understand?'

The Bogle grinned and plunged on

58

through the mist. He began to sing in a cheese-grater voice, and soon the swirling mists drew apart and they struggled out on to dry land. The sun was shining, the marsh was behind them and there was Hubert, sitting behind a large canvas with a big brushful of grey-green paint at the ready.

The royal painter looked so terrified you might well have thought he'd seen a Bogle beasty, which he had, so no wonder. But Belinda climbed down from the Bogle's back and told Hubert the whole story, and at the end they even shook hands. Hubert was still holding his big paintbrush, which was rather unfortunate for Knackerleevee, but he said he didn't mind since he was practically that colour anyway.

They were just thinking of sitting down and opening the packed lunches they'd brought on the cart when there was a cheerful shout from a nearby rock and the Princess Saramanda popped up her pretty head, all a-glitter with diamonds.

'Yoohoo!' she cried ever so sweetly. 'Belinda! Look behind you!'

Belinda glanced over her shoulder. 'Oh dear,' she murmured.

Waiting behind them, and armed to the teeth with swords and bows and real guns that went *bang!* if you pulled the triggers, were Saramanda's cut-throat robbers. There were only nine of them, as the others were still in hospital, and some of the nine had their arms in slings or were propped up on crutches.

Nevertheless they were there, and they would not come any closer. They pointed their guns with a great deal of menace while Saramanda explained the situation.

'Really, Belinda, it is most terribly kind of you to get this ugly Bogle beasty for me. King Krust is going to be *so* delighted. Do you know, he'll probably be so pleased he'll let me marry that deliciously handsome Bruno creature and then I shall have half a kingdom too.'

Saramanda fluttered her long eyelashes and sighed at the thought of it all. 'Now my cut-throat robbers, take this smelly mattress on legs and tie him to the cart. When you've done that you can take these two back into the marsh – and make sure they never come out!'

6

Hubert is artful

Belinda watched helplessly while Knackerleevee was forced to the old cart. The wary
robbers kept their distance. They had learnt
their lesson and they knew that if they came
too close to either the Bogle or Belinda there
would be trouble. So they stayed safely a few
paces away, waving their swords and guns.

Belinda felt very sorry for Knackerleevee.
Things had taken quite an unexpected turn,
and there was no telling what would happen
to the Bogle when Saramanda turned up at
the castle. She watched sadly as the cart
jerked forwards and slowly rumbled away
down the track and out of sight, with the
Bogle bound and gagged and stuffed beneath
some old canvases of Hubert's.

Belinda and Hubert had their own problems, for the nine remaining robbers were
obviously looking forward to carrying out
Saramanda's orders. The new leader (you
will remember that the old one was left stuck
up a tree) was a fine fellow, a good five feet

tall and wearing a black hat with a rim so enormous you could have filled it with water and sailed little boats round it. He also wore big black boots and he kept his swords, any number of them, stuffed down the insides. If he took his boots off, you would have seen his feet were covered in plasters.

The other robbers were all grinning madly and wriggling their swords and guns and muttering dark threats.

'Chop off their heads!'

'No – chop off their ears!'

'Chop everything. Chip, chop, chop the lot!'

Belinda had heard it all before, but last time she had been able to save herself with a display of karate. It didn't seem as if she would have the chance this time and she was quite at a loss to know what to do. She whispered to Hubert beside her.

'I'm sorry for getting you into this mess.'

Hubert stared glumly at his unfinished painting of Belinda fighting the Bogle. He wished that he could do something for once, but all he could do was paint pictures of kings and important people. He couldn't fight, not even to save his life. He wasn't at all brave. Sometimes the royal painter hated himself.

The robber chief swaggered up to Belinda and stuck a knife under her chin. 'Come on,

Your Most Royal Royal Highness. We've got to take a little walk. This way!'

Hubert suddenly jumped forward and grabbed the robber's arm. 'Stop a moment. Hold it . . . That's it! Fantastic!' The robber chief half closed one eye and glared at Hubert.

'What are you playing at?' he growled.

The royal painter slowly shook his head and murmured, 'Such a fine head! When you moved just now you looked so strong and powerful. It really should be painted.' Hubert stroked the robber chief's bristly beard. 'Magnificent. Think how it would look on canvas, with a big gold frame round it. Such a head!'

By this time the robber chief was looking considerably less angry and was preening his beard thoughtfully. 'Of course I look magnificent,' he declared. 'I'm a cut-throat robber chief.'

Hubert clasped his hands together. 'Please,' he began, 'please let me paint your portrait before I die. I've always wanted to paint a picture of somebody marvellous, somebody whose face really shows strength of character and brave resolve. You have just that face . . .'

Two of the other robbers pushed Hubert roughly to one side.

'If he's going to paint you, then he's going to paint all of us. We'll all have our picture painted, won't we, lads?'

'Oh yes!' cried Belinda. 'Do paint them all, Hubert. They're such a fine-looking bunch of fellows.'

Now all the robbers began to lick their fingers and tidy their hair. They brushed the dry mud from their breeches and tucked their shirts in. Hubert began to organize them into a little group. The robber chief was still mighty suspicious, but he was desperate to have his portrait done by a real, royal artist. He stood very stiff and pompous in the middle of his gang and pointed his gun at Princess Belinda.

'Don't you get any funny ideas, Princess, or this gun will go off and you'll go off with it.'

Belinda smiled and replied, 'I wouldn't dream of it.' And she winked at Hubert. The painter set up his easel and canvas and selected his paints. Then he began to paint. He worked quickly, slapping the colours on and working them deftly with master-strokes of the brush. The robbers began to shift about nervously, dying to know what their picture looked like. Hubert threw the brush over his shoulder.

'Finished!' he cried. There was a mad

charge as the robbers dashed round to the other side of the easel to see their portrait. Hubert carefully withdrew.

There was a great roar of laughter, and another one of rage. 'Ha, ha! Look at the chief's ear. It looks like a cabbage.'

'It *is* a cabbage. It is a cabbage, and look at his nose. It's all purple and blue. And look, look, that's you at the back there.'

'Where? That's not me.'

'Of course it is. Your nose looks just like that cucumber!'

'My nose isn't like a cucumber. That's you – don't you even recognize yourself? If you don't recognize the nose, you can tell by those crossed eyes. I've never seen anybody as cross-eyed as you in my life.'

'Me cross-eyed! Who are you calling cross-eyed, you mouldy cucumber snout? I'll make you cross-eyed!' Out came the swords and soon the nine cut-throat robbers were hard at it, slicing each other up and poking and prodding and biffing and baffing until there was so much dust they would never have seen Belinda and Hubert slowly creep away even if they had stopped for a moment.

The princess and the painter found the robbers' horses tied to some nearby trees. Belinda jumped up into the saddle and called to Hubert.

'Come on, hurry!'

'I can't ride. I've never ridden a horse in all my life.'

Belinda pulled her mount round and rode to Hubert. 'It's very easy,' she explained. 'You sit on its back and put one leg on each side and hold on tight.'

'I know that!' snapped Hubert. 'I'm not stupid. How do I get up on to it?'

'You think about nine robbers about to stick their swords into you and jump!'

Hardly were the words out of her mouth than Hubert was up on a horse, wobbling a little and facing the tail, but still in the saddle. Belinda held the horse steady while Hubert turned himself round. Then she released all the other horses and shooed them away, so that they went off at a gallop, leaving the robbers with a transport problem.

Hubert and Belinda then set off at a gallop themselves, determined to catch up with the cheating Saramanda before she reached the palace and claimed both prince and half the kingdom for herself. Hubert had a very hard time of it and he felt as if he were trying to control a high-speed earthquake. He was so shaken and jarred he was quite certain that by the time he reached the palace all his bones would be lying in tiny fragments at the bottom of his boots and the palace guards would have to tip him out on to the floor when he arrived.

Everything seemed to do its best to slow them down. First of all Hubert forgot to hold on to his reins and did a wonderful backward somersault over the horse's tail to land in the hard dust. Then he forgot to press his knees against the horse's sides and bounced so high he landed almost on the horse's head – and the horse wasn't at all pleased about that. Then they went galloping through a wood and no fewer than five tree branches whopped the poor painter in the stomach or on the head and knocked him flying from his panting mount.

At last Belinda gave up and declared that he would have to sit behind her and hold on tight. By this time Hubert was only semi-conscious, and it was the only thing he was capable of doing anyway.

With the extra weight they could not make much speed, and they had to stop frequently

to let the poor horse regain some strength. Eventually they trotted up a long rise, and when they reached the top they saw King Krust's castle in front of them, on the far side of the plain.

Belinda could just make out a puff of dust crawling towards the great castle wall. Even as she watched, the distant cart stopped at the gates.

'Well,' muttered Belinda, 'she's got there before us. But I'm not giving up yet.' She urged the horse down the hill towards the glittering castle.

7

A princely prize

Princess Saramanda Sneak entered the castle in triumph. King Krust himself came hurrying down the castle's great stairway, almost tripping over his real fox-fur robe in his rush to greet the princess. She waited at the bottom of the stairs, her eyes bright with success and her heart black with cheating.

The king had to stand on the bottom step to say hallo, and even then Saramanda was taller than he was.

'You were so quick!' cried King Krust. Then he spied the red paint on her dress. 'Are you hurt? Are you wounded? Are you all right?'

The princess gave a little shrug. 'It's nothing. Just a flesh wound. The Bogle must have scratched me as I threw him over my shoulder.'

The king's eyes rolled right round and back to where they started. 'You threw the Bogle over your shoulder? Goodness, such strength. Bruno will be delighted.' The king gave her a sly grin. 'He's been practising, you know.'

At that moment Prince Bruno de Bruno Bunkum Krust himself made a guest appearance. He stood at the top of the stairs, his firm jaw jutting out firmly, his shoulders bulging with overworked muscles beneath his dapper tunic and his half-closed eyes resting lazily on the company below.

Most of the ladies-in-waiting swooned at the mere sight of so handsome a creature. He came slowly down the stairs, his sword clinking at his side, until he finally reached the bottom step and stood in front of the Princess Saramanda, eyeing her carefully.

'Ah,' he drawled. 'So you are Saramanda. My father has told me all about you. He is quite right. You're very beautiful. I hear you threw the Bogle over your shoulder.'

The princess smiled sweetly and curtsied. 'Yes,' and she blushed prettily and added, 'I'm afraid my dress got a little blood on it.'

The prince studied the paint stains gravely. 'Indeed. You must find a lady-in-waiting and have it seen to. Then we shall discuss the wedding.' Bruno leant forward and took Saramanda's hand and kissed it.

'Just a minute, just a minute,' interrupted

the king. 'We haven't even seen this Bogle yet. Where is this horrible monster? Is it dead or alive?'

'I have it in the cart, Your Majesty.'

'Oh, fine fine. Bring in the cart!' roared King Krust. The huge doors were pushed open and Hubert's old cart was rolled into the hall. 'Isn't that Hubert's cart?' asked the king. 'I wonder what happened to him.'

Saramanda bent close to the king's ear and whispered. 'I'm afraid he was rather frightened by all the roaring and he ran away. I don't know where he went.'

King Krust patted her hand. 'Don't worry, my dear. Plenty more royal painters where he came from. Never did like him much. He always painted the queen's nose too large and made me sit quite still for hours, you know. Hours and hours. I used to get pins and needles in my erhum, you know, my . . .'

'Oh yes!' cried Saramanda. 'I know.' The king nodded with great seriousness.

Then the old canvas cover was pulled from the cart and there was Knackerleevee, peacefully snoring away at the bottom of the cart with his legs tied to his arms and his arms tied to his legs. In fact, there was so much rope and hair he looked like a giant ball of wool, very badly wound.

Everybody gathered round and stared at the famous monster from the Marsh at the End of the World. King Krust borrowed a guard's spear and gave the Bogle a little poke. 'Are you sure it's alive?' he asked the princess.

Bruno de Bruno was holding his nose and waving one hand in front of his face. 'I say, it's a bit of a strong pong, isn't it?'

Somebody suggested that the Bogle looked like a mouldy old carpet and smelled like one too. Everybody began to lean forward and poke the helpless creature, and eventually Knackerleevee must have begun to feel something through his thick hide because he opened one pink eye and glared out through the sides of the cart. Then he snorted and tried to stretch himself. Finding himself all bound up, he suddenly remembered what had befallen him.

Now, Knackerleevee may have been ugly and dirty and smelly and not too clever, but he was proud. So he didn't lose his temper or

growl or roar and spit. He just lowered his head once more and stared back at all the people staring at him.

King Krust was disappointed. 'It doesn't look very fierce,' he ventured.

'That's because I tied him up,' said Saramanda. The Bogle watched the princess thoughtfully, thinking that she was the one who had caused all the trouble.

'Was it a terrible fight?' asked Bruno, peering closely at Knackerleevee's long fingernails.

'He was very strong,' said Saramanda,

leaning against the cart. 'But I beat him in the end,' and she smiled.

The Bogle suddenly heaved himself upright, with a roaring splutter that was half laughter and half anger. 'That daisy-faced-little-bitty-pretty-pretty princess! Beat me? She couldn't squeeze a lemon! Do you think she fought me? Is that what she's told you? I'll tell you what . . .'

But King Krust had got his spear and poked it angrily at the Bogle. The king's face was quite red. 'How dare you speak like that to a princess! Don't you dare to call her

daisy-faced – or she'll throw you over her shoulder again.'

'Ha! She couldn't throw a banana skin, let alone me. I'm Knackerleevee the Bogle, and nobody, nobody, gets the better of me except . . .'

'Don't listen to him,' cried Saramanda. 'He's just being nasty because he lost the fight.'

Knackerleevee gave a low growl and tried to get away from the little pin pricks of the king's spear. 'It was Belinda who beat me, and I don't mind telling you. She's the strongest and the kindest person I have ever met. As for this glittering thing here – she's a cheat and a liar.'

Prince Bruno de Bruno rushed up to the cart and rattled the sides furiously. 'Don't you dare speak to my future wife like that, you overgrown fungus. Apologize at once!'

Knackerleevee glared at the prince with his pink eyes and snorted. 'Go away and do your press-ups, you overgrown muscle.'

Then everybody began to speak and shout and yell at once. The hall was in uproar, and in the midst of it all there was a clatter of hooves and Belinda and Hubert came riding right into the hall. Princess Belinda gave a cry of delight as she spotted the Bogle.

'Knackerleevee! You're all right! Oh, I am glad.'

'Guards, surround that princess!' yelled Bruno de Bruno, quite white with fury. There was a clatter of armour and the guards rushed up and around Belinda's prancing horse.

She gazed calmly down at them. 'I think I can guess what's been happening,' she mused. 'Saramanda has told you her story.'

The prince stiffened. 'Quite right, and I intend to marry her in the morning!'

Belinda looked at Knackerleevee and the king waving his spear about as if he were the bravest king in the world. She saw the demure Saramanda with her sweet, innocent smile, and she saw Bruno de Bruno, tall, straight and idiotically handsome. She began to laugh. She laughed and slowly shook her head from side to side. After all the things she'd been through – fighting cut-throat robbers, wading through marshes, bonking guards and everything else she'd done to marry Bruno – she suddenly realized he was a fool.

Princess Saramanda frowned for the first time in this story. 'She's gone mad!' she said. 'She's making it all up. Guards, take her away!'

Then Belinda stopped laughing, for Knackerleevee was still bound to the cart and she had unfinished business. As the guards pressed forward, Belinda slipped down from the horse and faced them. Hubert shut his eyes. He was beginning to feel rather sorry for the palace guards. He couldn't bear to watch, but he heard the thuds and groans and moans. He heard the screech of armour as it clanged against the walls of the hall. He heard the yells and screams as one by one and two by two the guards were put out of action.

Meanwhile Knackerleevee sat in the cart and grunted with satisfaction, a broad grin on his hairy face. King Krust, Saramanda and Bruno did a slow retreat up the staircase, and by the time Belinda had laid out the last guard they were on the balcony. Belinda climbed into the cart and untied her Bogle companion. Knackerleevee stretched his arms and legs and rubbed his chest.

'You said you'd teach me,' he reminded Belinda.

'I will, I will. Now, come with me. We have one more thing to do.' She got down from the cart and ran lightly up the stairs.

'Don't run away, brave king!' she cried after the disappearing royals. 'I know it wasn't your fault, and I mean you no harm.'

The king stopped and came creeping sheepishly back. 'I think you can see now that it was I who defeated the Bogle.'

King Krust nodded anxiously. 'And so I claim my prize,' said Belinda evenly. 'Marriage to Prince Bruno de Bruno and half the kingdom.'

At this the prince stepped forward as if to protest, but Knackerleevee rushed forward, seized the prince by the collar and dangled him over the balcony. 'Don't say a word,' hissed the Bogle, 'or you'll wish you knew how to fly!' Bruno's open mouth shut with a loud snap.

Saramanda looked as white as a ghost. Just when she thought she'd succeeded too. King Krust turned to her and shrugged. 'What can I do?' he murmured.

Belinda gave a little smile. 'I'll tell you what you can do. I have passed the test and so I win Bruno and half the kingdom. Fine. I now wish to give Bruno away. I don't think he'll be at all suitable. Saramanda can have him and I hope they'll be very happy.' Knackerleevee's eyes boggled in disbelief. 'As for half the kingdom,' said Belinda evenly. 'I'll have the half with the diamond mine, thank you very much.' King Krust almost had a heart attack at this, so Belinda turned to the marble balcony and raised her arm.

'Haaa–AKK!' there was a splinter of breaking stone and half the balcony plummeted down to the hall floor and shattered.

'Yes, yes, yes!' cried the king. 'The half with the diamond mine! That's fine – lovely! Oh, how wonderful! What a dear, sweet, kind, beautiful, beautiful princess you are,' he cried, now down on his knees and kissing Belinda's hand rapturously.

Belinda grinned down at Hubert. 'Come on then, you two,' she cried cheerfully. 'Let's be off to our new kingdom. I need a good bodyguard. In fact, you can be my army, Knackerleevee. And Hubert can come and paint pictures of my new kingdom for me. And I shall send for Hiro Ono to teach you karate, Knackerleevee. My parents may even come to tea – you never know!'

They went down to the old cart, hitched up the horse, climbed on board and trundled out of the palace, leaving King Krust still on his knees, Saramanda and Bruno staring at each other with stupefied grins on their faces and thirty-eight guards lying unconscious on the floor with large dents all over their armour.

The karate princess had made her mark.